Vanina Starkoff

Along the River

Translated by Jane Springer

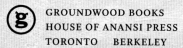

GROUNDWOOD BOOKS
HOUSE OF ANANSI PRESS
TORONTO   BERKELEY

The phrase "More love, please" *(Mais amor, por favor)* links up with
the "poetic action" project that brings poetry into public spaces,
funded by Mexican poet Armando Alanis Pulido.

Groundwood Books / House of Anansi Press
groundwoodbooks.com

With the participation of the Government of Canada
Avec la participation du gouvernement du Canada | Canadä

Library and Archives Canada Cataloguing in Publication
Starkoff, Vanina
[Pelo rio. English]
Along the river / Vanina Starkoff ; Jane Springer, translator.
Translation of: Pelo rio.
Issued in print and electronic formats.
ISBN 978-1-55498-977-5 (hardback). —
ISBN 978-1-55498-978-2 (pdf)
I. Springer, Jane, translator II. Title. III. Title: Pelo rio. English
PZ7.S79555Al 2017   j869.3'5   C2016-904228-6
C2016-904229-4

The illustrations were painted in acrylic, then digitized and finished
in Photoshop.
Printed and bound in Malaysia

For all the wonderful people I met on the river …

Everyone travels along the river ...

HAPPiNESS School

BEAUTiFul Smile

… by ship or boat or canoe.

My HEART

EVERYTHiNG iS Good HERE

You will have to search for …

... your own way

and your own rhythm ...

… while continuing to steer your course.

Springs,

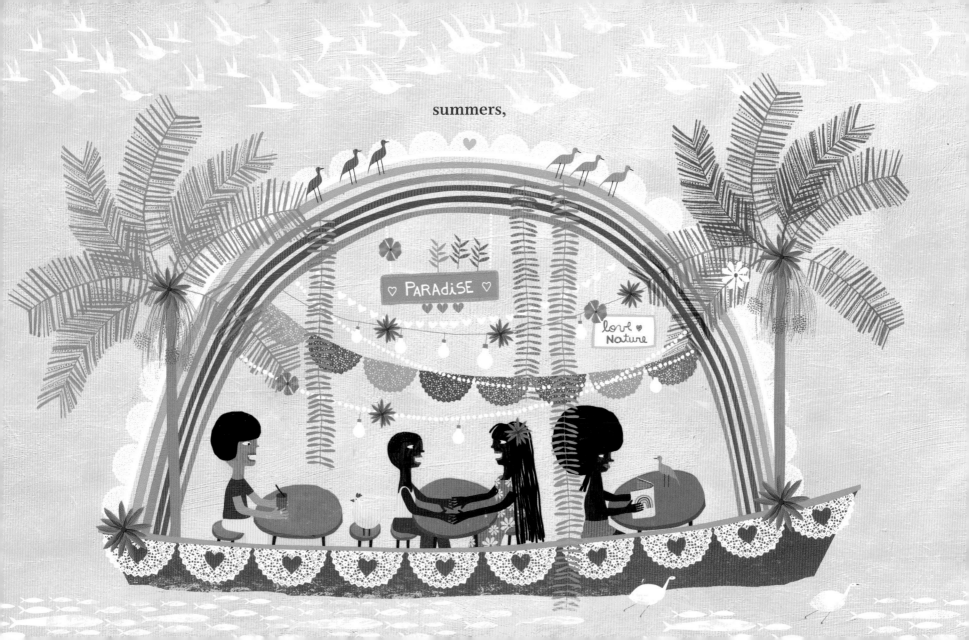

summers,

falls and winters …

… you'll live through them all.

And yes, as you're sailing along the river, you will long to reach the sea.

Surely the wind will be at your back.

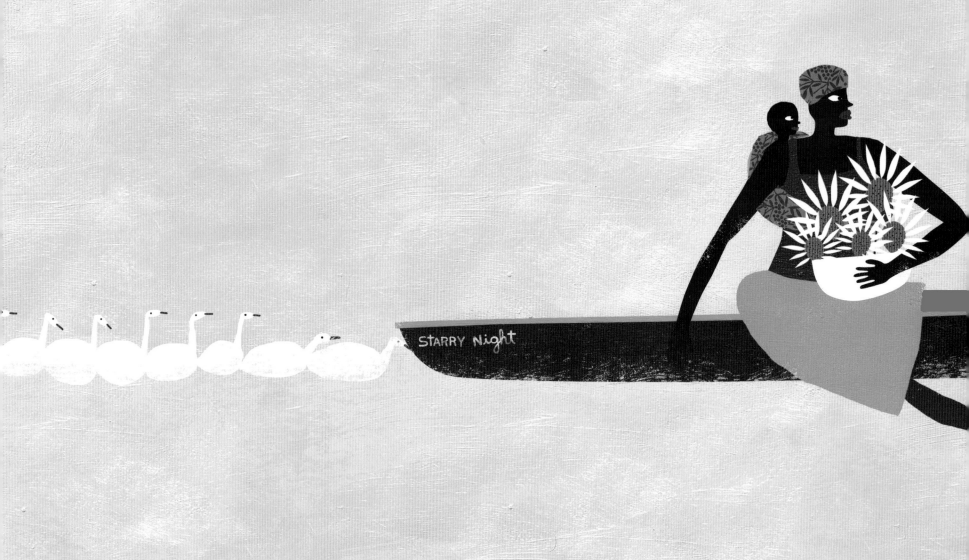

Along the river or on the sea, you will have to discover …

ALONG THE RIVER

I AM HAPPY

… your own way and your own rhythm …

... while never letting go of your dreams.